Hostage

Hostage

ALEX KROPP

HIP Xtreme Novels

NATIONAL LIBRARY OF CANADA CATALOGUING IN PUBLICATION DATA
Kropp, Alex, 1979–
    Hostage / Alex Kropp.

ISBN 978-1-926847-29-0

    I. Title.

PS8621.R66H68 2012   jC81'.6   C2011-908540-2

General editor: Paul Kropp
Text Design: Laura Brady
Illustrations by: Charlie Hnatiuk
Cover design: Robert Corrigan

1 2 3 4 5 6 7   17 16 15 14 13 12

Printed and bound in Canada

High Interest Publishing acknowledges the financial support of the Government of Canada through the Canada Book Fund for our publishing activities.

Rob was just going to the bank to put in some money. He didn't expect a bank robbery. He didn't expect to become a hostage. But now he needs all his smarts just to stay alive.

Contents

Chapter 1

Because of Mom

We'd have never been in the bank that day – except for my mom. My mom has this thing about money, maybe because we don't have any. She makes me put half of what I make in the bank. "It all adds up," she says.

My mom is right about that. I make money doing yard work, painting walls, and sometimes babysitting. I call myself "Anything for a Buck, Inc.," except that I'm just a kid who does odd jobs. The day I went into the bank, I had $466.74 in my savings account and another $25 to deposit. Grand total of $491.74. I might hit $700 by the end of the summer. Maybe enough to buy a car when I left school. That was my plan.

The plan was coming along fine, until that Saturday. That day at the bank. The day Peeps and I became hostages. The day I almost got killed.

"Dude, you can't bring a baseball bat into a bank," I told my buddy Peeps. Peeps (short for Pedro) was standing on the sidewalk with a metal bat. We were on our way to play baseball, and Peeps has the good metal baseball bat.

"Why not?" he asked.

"Because they'll think you're a bank robber," I told him.

"Yeah, Rob. That's real smart. Like bank robbers hold up banks with baseball bats all the time."

"I'm just saying. Somebody might call the cops, and then you'd have to explain, and then. . . ."

"Okay, I'll stay back by the door," he said. "You go put your money in."

So the two of us walked inside. I guess I could have used the bank machine to make the deposit. I mean, it was only $25. But I kind of like seeing the numbers go up in my bank book. That's the whole point, isn't it?

Besides, the line was pretty short. There was only one woman ahead of me, and she looked like she was in a hurry. I'd go up to the teller right after her and put my money in. Then we'd be off to play some ball.

Easy peasy. That's always what Peeps says when he makes a good catch. Easy peasy.

Besides, I had one more reason to wait in line. Kate was at the counter. Beautiful, sexy Kate was at the counter.

Our local bank has maybe six different tellers. Most of them are old and most of them are ugly. But Kate is something else. She's in her 20s with blonde hair, blue eyes and a body. . . . Let's just say I'd come to the bank to make a two-cent deposit when Kate's working.

"Your lucky day, Rob," Peeps told me. He saw where I was looking. "She's here."

"Guess so."

"Just don't drool on your bank book," he said. "It's not cool. Makes you look like a loser."

"Right."

"Even if you are a loser," he mumbled.

No reason to reply to that. I went forward and got in line.

Sometimes I wish I were five years older, and Kate were five years younger. But that's just a dream. Right now I'm a pimply teenage kid and she's a blonde goddess. I'm a kid with a few hundred bucks in the bank and she's a hot 20-year-old blonde.

Peeps is right – I haven't got a chance.

Even worse, I never made it to Kate's counter. The lady in front of me went to Kate. And then old Mrs. Dutton opened up beside her. I kind of like Mrs. Dutton. She's pretty cool for an old lady, and she knows me and my mom. But there's no thrill, if you know what I mean.

"Hi, Rob," Mrs. Dutton said. "Made some money this weekend?"

"Yeah, a little," I said.

"Garden work?"

"Nah," I told her. Then I dropped my voice so Kate wouldn't hear. "Babysitting."

"Well, it's a job," she said.

"Yeah, guess so," I said. I swiped my card, gave her my bank book and the $25.

She began typing something into her computer. Then she looked up. "Good news, Rob. You made 22 cents interest."

"Whoo-ee! I'm rich."

"Well, it all adds up."

I was thinking that all moms must go to school to learn the same stuff. "It all adds up." "Wash your hands before you eat." "Get out of bed and get to school." Some day I'll do a whole book of mom-stuff. I'll call mine *Things Moms Always Tell You.* It'll be a bestseller, for sure.

Mrs. Dutton had just gone to put my bank book in the printer when there was a noise at the door. At first, I thought Peeps had dropped the baseball bat. But I was wrong.

I turned to the door and saw two guys come in. They moved fast, pushing Peeps into the bank, shutting the door behind them. It took me a second to see that they both had stockings over their heads.

That was bad.

And both of them had guns.

That was worse.

"Stay cool," barked the taller guy. "Stay cool and nobody gets hurt."

I put up my hands. So did Mrs. Dutton. Peeps dropped the baseball bat and he put up his hands.

"Okay, let's have the cash," the guy shouted. He went up to Kate and pointed the gun at her.

Kate's hands were shaking when she reached into the till. She pulled out a fistful of money and handed it over.

"You, old bag," the robber shouted at Mrs. Dutton. He put out his hand, waiting for money.

Mrs. Dutton did the same as Kate. She gave him a fistful of cash.

The robber looked at the money. I guess he didn't like what he saw.

"This is nothing," he shouted. "We didn't come in here for a couple hundred bucks. Where's the real money?"

"In . . . in . . . the safe," Kate told him. She was so scared she could hardly talk.

"Well, get it," the robber ordered.

"We can't. Only the manager – "

Our bank is pretty small. The manager has the only office, off to the side. It has one window on the bank and one window on the street. The manager sat in there behind a desk. He wasn't looking out toward us.

"Let's get him out here," said the robber. He went over to the office and kicked open the door. "You," he shouted, "out here. Get that safe open, now."

The bank manager came out, looking scared. He was a pretty old guy, maybe forty or so. He also had his hands up in the air. He was trying to explain something to the robbers. There was a time lock on the safe, he said. Only so much money could come out at one time. Or something like that.

The robber didn't like what he said. He lifted his gun to one side and then smashed it into the bank manager's face.

Suddenly there was blood. Lots of it.

"I said open it," the tall robber repeated.

The bank manager couldn't speak. His mouth was dripping blood.

"Open it!" the robber barked.

Silently, the manager walked over to the safe. He began typing something into a computer.

In another minute, maybe, the safe might have opened. The two robbers would have gotten the money they wanted. They'd have gone running out the door to a getaway car. And then we'd have hung around to tell the police what we saw.

If we'd been lucky, the safe would have opened faster. Or the cops would have been slower.

Outside, there was a siren. A flashing light. And then another siren.

The cops were outside.

The tall robber swore. "All of you, inside the office. Now. Like now. Nobody's going no place."

Chapter 2

Hostages

Was I scared? Kind of, but I felt more weird than scared. It was like I was in a movie. The movie was going on all around me, but it was like I had no control over myself. Like I was trapped in a bad dream. There were robbers, with guns, and me and Peeps and the bank people. And we were all scared, all ready to burst into tears.

So did I pinch myself and wake up? I couldn't. This was real. This was a nightmare, but it was real.

"You, zit-face, move it!" The tall robber was talking to me. I guess I wasn't moving fast enough.

That's one more thing a mom should tell you. Never argue when a guy is pointing a gun at you. Now that would be good advice.

"I'm moving," I wanted to say, but the words stuck in my throat.

Silently, I followed the others inside the office. There were six of us. Three worked for the bank – the manager, Mrs. Dutton and Kate. Three of us were just people – Peeps, the woman in a hurry and me. That gave the robbers six hostages. They would trade us for a chance to escape. Simple as that.

If the cops were willing to make a trade.

"Okay. On the floor. All of you," the robber ordered.

So we all sat down on the floor.

The bank manager's office wasn't large. Along one wall there was a big desk and two chairs. That left two inner walls and the window wall for us. Peeps and I took the inside wall. The three bank people took the wall with the windows. The woman in a hurry sat across from us. The two robbers stood at the door.

"Watch 'em," said the tall robber. Then he went out to the tellers' counters.

Outside it was silent. No more sirens. We knew the cops were out there, but we couldn't hear a thing.

The short robber stood there with his gun pointed at us. He said nothing. He hadn't said anything since the two of them burst into the bank.

So it was quiet, but then Kate began to cry. She was shaking, and trying hard not to make a sound. But tears began falling down her cheeks.

Mrs. Dutton reached out and took Kate's hand.

"It'll be okay," the manager told her.

"Shut up!" the short robber barked at us. I could tell by his voice that he was young, maybe not much older than me. And I think he was scared, too. You can hear that in a voice when it goes high and shaky.

Maybe the kid robber was as scared as we were, even though he had a gun.

The manager shot a nasty look at the young robber. Mrs. Dutton was looking at him, too. Both their looks told the kid that he should be ashamed.

But the kid wasn't buying it. He was staring at Kate and her really short skirt. Then he looked at his gun, and then at the bank manager.

Outside, we could hear the other robber, the older one. That guy was talking to somebody, maybe on his cell phone.

"Yeah, you took off. . . . No way, I'm not blaming you. . . . You could've . . . Well, I don't know . . . Yeah, you know where to go. . . . We're gonna get some real money out of this. . . . Yeah, like that's it."

The call must have gone to a third guy, a driver. Maybe the driver took off when the cops showed up. It was hard to tell just by listening to one side of the phone call. The three robbers must have had a plan at first. Maybe a quick bank robbery, then a quick getaway. If the cops hadn't shown up, maybe it would have worked. But now the driver was going somewhere to meet the two robbers later.

If the two robbers made it out of the bank. If the

police let them go. If nothing else went wrong.

Outside, I heard a sliding noise. The tall robber must have been going through the tellers' money drawers. He must have taken the $25 I had just put in. He probably got a lot more.

Then the phone on the manager's desk rang.

"Al, the phone," shouted the kid.

"I know it's the freakin' phone," the old robber shot back. "Now shut up." He must have been angry that the kid used his name.

"You gonna answer it?" the kid asked. "Maybe it's the cops."

There was a pause while Al thought about it. Then he came into the office and grabbed the phone. Again, I got only one side of it.

"Yeah. —— Nice to talk to you, Officer Doyle. You having a busy day there at the cop shop? —— Oh, you're right outside. I never would have freakin' guessed. But maybe the sirens were a clue. Let me give you a little advice. If you guys wanted to sneak up on us, turn off the sirens. It works better."

I bet Al was smiling under his stocking. He seemed pretty cool about all this. Maybe he'd been through it before.

"Yeah, we've got some hostages in here. —— Let me count. Yeah, six of 'em. Nobody's hurt yet, except one guy with a mouth problem. —— No reason for nobody to get hurt. —— You get us a car, we give you the hostages. No problem."

There was another pause while Al listened. I guess Officer Doyle had a whole bunch to say. It was quite a while before Al replied.

"Yeah, thanks for the offer, but no thanks. You check with your boss and get us a car. Don't try busting through the door or you'll have a bunch of dead people here. That won't look good on your resumé, Doyle. Bunch of dead bodies and you'll never get a desk job."

Kate began crying again. This time, nobody said anything.

"You call me back when you get the car," Al said to the phone. "Otherwise we got nothing to talk about." And then he hung up.

Again it was quiet. All we could hear was Kate sniffling.

"Don't you get all worried, cute stuff," Al said to her. "You'll be the last one to get a bullet, that's for sure. We always start with the ugly ones first."

Then he laughed. I guess he figured that line was pretty funny.

"Okay, you, manager guy," Al went on. "What's your name?"

"Mr. Morton," he said. His name came out funny because of the big cut on his lip.

"How about we drop the 'mister' and just call you Morton?" Al said to him. He looked above the manager's desk and saw a photograph. It showed Mr. Morton with a dark-haired wife and two kids. "Nice family you got. I suppose you'd like to see them again some time."

"Yeah," Mr. Morton said.

"So that means you got to open the safe," Al told him. "Simple as that. You get some real money out of that safe, and you get to go home and see the family. Fair deal? All these people get to go home. But you got to open the safe first."

"I understand," Mr. Morton said.

"So come on out here and do what you gotta do," Al told him.

"Just so long as nobody gets hurt," the bank manager said.

"My buddy and me, we don't like to hurt people, do

we?" Al said. He looked at the other robber.

Mr. Morton touched his bleeding lip. I don't think he believed what Al said.

The robber pointed his gun at Mr. Morton. "A lot of people are depending on you. But you can do it, Morton. We're all counting on you."

Chapter 3

Heating Up

It was getting warm inside the manager's office. I was sweating like crazy. I could feel the sweat building up in my armpits. I could only guess what I smelled like.

Everybody else looked hot, too. Peeps was sweating so much his T-shirt was soaked. Old Mrs. Dutton had sweat on her face. The lady in a hurry had taken off her jacket. Even Kate – the perfect Kate – was red in the face. She seemed very warm.

For the robber whose head was in a stocking, it must have been awful.

"Why don't you take off the stocking?" I suggested.

"Shut up," he barked.

"Well, it's hot," I said. "But you suit yourself." I thought that sounded almost friendly. I mean, he had a gun and all, but it was still hot in the room.

The heat seemed to get worse after I mentioned it. In five minutes, the kid shouted out to his buddy. "Hey, can I take this freakin' sock off?"

The buddy didn't answer.

And then something crazy happened. The kid looked in the corner of the office. There was a camera up there – a video camera that taped all of us. I saw the kid look at the camera, then call out to his buddy.

"Hey, Al."

Again, no answer.

So the kid lifted his gun and aimed it at the camera.

Kapow!

One shot and the camera was toast.

Whoa, the kid is a good shot, I thought. I could smell the smoke from the gun. I could feel the sound of the shot bouncing around in my head.

The kid laughed and pulled off his stocking. "I hate cameras," he said.

At last we could see his face. The kid robber really was just a kid, maybe 16 or 17. He was zit-faced, like me, with a small mouth and buck teeth. His hair was

dark and messed up from the stocking. His eyes were blue and a little bloodshot.

Suddenly Al came to the door. "What happened?" Al asked.

"Nothing," the kid told him. "It's getting hot, so I took off this freakin' stocking. I figured I better take out the camera first."

"I thought you shot somebody," Al said.

"Nah. Not yet," the kid replied. Then he laughed.

I really didn't like the laugh. It was kind of crazy. If you think about it, shooting a video camera is crazy too, but the laugh was worse. It was like this kid could do anything. He could shoot Peeps, or me, or Kate and then laugh about it. He was that crazy.

Or so I thought.

"Okay," Al told him, "but no more shooting unless I say so. Or unless . . . you have to."

"Yeah, gotcha," the kid replied.

The telephone rang. Al picked it up. He kept one eye on the other room. I guess he didn't want Mr. Morton to make a break for it.

"Yeah . . ." he answered. "No problem. —— Yeah, I know there was a gunshot, but my buddy was just practicing. He's a little trigger happy. —— No, nobody got shot. Make that, nobody got shot yet. —— So where is that freakin' car?"

There was a pause. I guess the cops on the other end of the line were explaining. Al had a look on his face like he didn't believe them.

"It's coming? So's Christmas. —— You got half an hour, then somebody gets hurt. —— Oh, you want to change the deal? You want what?"

There was a long pause. Al seemed to be listening hard. Then he put the phone down and checked on the bank manager. After that, he got back on the phone.

"Okay, we maybe don't need all these guys," Al told him. "It's getting kind of hot and sweaty in here, so you can have one of them. That make you happy?"

There was a long pause.

"Nah, I'm not giving you two. No way. Just one, to show what nice guys we are."

The cop must have said something on the other side. Then Al replied, "And don't forget the freakin' car. We do our part of the deal, you do yours."

Al hung up the phone. There was an awkward minute of two. He looked down at us. We looked up at him. It was as though he were making up his mind. One hostage was going to go free. Which one? Al seemed to be asking himself that question.

"Okay, so which one of you gets out of here?" Al asked. He had a strange smile on his face. "Which one of you wants to stay alive . . . the most?"

Chapter 4

The Contest

So that was the trade. The cops give the robbers a car. The robbers give up one hostage. It was a pretty simple trade. Later, they'd probably let the rest of us go.

Probably.

If nothing went wrong.

If the cops didn't go crazy.

If the kid robber didn't go crazy.

If nobody tried to make a break for it.

That was an awful lot of ifs. No wonder I was sweating so much – it wasn't just the heat.

"So one of you gets to leave early," Al told us. "The kid here is going to pick one of you to go for a walk outside. It's a little contest. You tell the kid why you get to go home. Make a good case for yourself, and you're out of here. Simple as that. But it's got to be quick."

Al looked at the kid, then added, "It's your pick. Make it good." Then he left and went back out with the bank manager.

The kid stood at the door, grinning.

"Okay, you heard it. We got a contest. One winner and four losers – and I'm the judge. Too bad we can't do this like *American Idol*, eh?" And then he laughed. This was a guy who liked his own jokes.

"You start," he said, pointing the gun at Peeps.

Peeps looked like a deer caught in the headlight of a car. His eyes were wide, his mouth half open – and he was frozen.

"I said you, Jose, or whatever your name is. You start."

"I . . . uh. . . ." Peeps began. "My name is Pedro, but everybody calls me Peeps, and I'm, uh, fifteen. And maybe I should go because . . . well, I don't know why. Maybe because I'm the youngest . . . but that sounds pretty stupid. I don't know. I never had to think about stuff like this – " and then his voice dropped off.

"That's all you got to say?" the robber asked.

Peeps nodded his head. That was it.

"Okay, you," the kid went on. He pointed the gun at the lady in a hurry, the one who had been ahead of me in line.

"Well, it should be me," the woman said. "I've got two kids, and one of them is waiting to get picked up from soccer practice. I should never have stopped at the bank. I was running late, and now my son is waiting, and he's not going to know where I am. . . ." Then she started crying. It was real crying, too, not the fake stuff.

"Okay, cut the tears, lady. It doesn't help."

"I've got to get out of here," the lady wailed. "I've got to. . . ."

The kid robber shook his head. He must be thinking that the contest was a bad idea.

"What about you?" he said, pointing the gun at me.

"Nobody's waiting for me," I told him. "Let the lady with the kids go. Or Mrs. Dutton, or Kate. I'll wait till the end."

"You some kind of hero?"

"No. I'm just trying to be fair," I said. "There's no point in letting me go. These other people . . . it matters more to them. Pick one of them, not me."

The kid robber swore. I didn't know if that was a good thing or a bad thing. Maybe he thought I was mouthing off. Who knows?

"What about you, teller lady?" the kid robber said to Mrs. Dutton.

Mrs. Dutton gave him a nasty look. "I can wait here, young man. Let the woman with the two children go outside."

"The customer comes first, eh?" the kid said. Then

he laughed again. Like I said, he enjoyed his own jokes.

Finally he pointed the gun at Kate. "What about you, hot stuff? Any reason I should let you go?"

Kate was shaking. I could feel how scared she was from the other side of the room. Her face was red and there were dried tears on her cheeks.

"No," she whispered.

"What's that?" the robber asked.

"No," Kate said a bit louder. "I'll stay."

"That's good," the robber told her. "I wasn't going to let you go anyhow. You're too good looking to leave right now."

Kate just shook her head. I don't know what she was thinking, except that she hated this guy.

"Okay, the judge is making up his mind. You or you . . . you or you," he said. He kept pointing the gun back and forth between Mrs. Dutton and the mom. "And I choose you, mom. So stop your crying and get up. You're going to walk out of here nice and slow. You tell the cops just how nice we are."

"Yes, yes I will," said the woman. "Thank you."

I thought that was a bit much, but who knows? Maybe she'd said the right thing. Or maybe the crying had actually worked. One thing was certain – she'd get out of this alive. The rest of us might end up dead.

"So you go out and see my buddy," the kid told her. "He'll tell you when to go. Keep your hands up in the air when you go out. Some of those cops are pretty trigger happy. No sense you getting shot, because they'd just blame us." He laughed a little, but then set his mouth firm. "So go. We get the car, and maybe one more gets to go. Maybe."

"Yes, sir," the woman said. The "sir" part must have stuck in her throat. This kid was a long way from being a "sir."

The woman got up and walked to the front of the bank. The other robber, Al, told her to go slow and not do anything funny. He'd have a gun on her back. If the cops tried anything funny, she'd get the first shot.

Peeps shot me a look. Maybe getting picked to go first wasn't the best thing.

I shrugged back at him.

The kid robber was watching the woman at the front of the bank. He really wasn't looking at us. Maybe that's why Peeps began mouthing something to me.

I gave him a look. I couldn't figure it out.

"B–a–t," he repeated, but not out loud. Peeps was

pointing at the baseball bat. It was just outside the office door. Then Peeps reached up with one hand, like he was going to scratch his head. But then he brought his hand down real fast, voom.

I got it. If we could get the bat, maybe we could take out one of these guys. But not two of them. It would only work if we could separate the two robbers.

"W–a–i–t," I mouthed back at him. We needed a plan. We needed surprise. We needed some way to get the two guys apart. We needed to get the bat and swing it hard and fast. But how?

Chapter 5

Waiting

Peeps was trying to say something else, but the kid turned to look at us.

He wasn't happy.

"I said no freakin' talking."

"Got it," Peeps said.

"You and hero over there," he said, pointing the gun at me, "don't even think about trying something. I know how to shoot this thing. I'd love to do some target practice on you, buddy." He was looking right at Peeps.

From the other room, we heard a door open and close. The lady customer was going outside. We all waited to see if there'd be a shot. But no, it was quiet.

So the mom with two kids was free. She was out of this nightmare. That left four of us in the office and the manager outside.

"One gone," the kid robber said. "Four to go."

"And the manager," I told him.

"Right, so make that five," the kid replied. "Thanks for fixing my freakin' math. You gonna be a school teacher?"

"Doesn't look like it," I told him. "I'm not that good at school."

"Me neither."

"So you rob banks instead?" I asked him.

"Yeah, I guess."

"Kind of dangerous work."

"You got that right."

For a second, you might think we were old buddies. Two guys talking about school and work and all that. But one guy had a gun and the other guy was sitting on the floor. One or both of them might end up dead. And they certainly weren't buddies.

Then the manager came in. He didn't say a word, just went to his desk and got a briefcase. He emptied out a lot of papers, then went back outside.

"Looks like you got your money," Peeps said.

"How do you know that?" the kid robber asked.

"The briefcase," Peeps told him. "Your buddy is going to put the money in a briefcase. That's how it works."

"Is that so?"

"Don't you ever watch movies?" Peeps went on. "You might get some tips on how to do this bank robbing stuff."

"Don't give me any lip," the kid robber shot back.

"Just an idea," Peeps told him.

"I said shut up," the robber told him. Then he pointed the gun in Peeps' direction.

We waited another five minutes in silence. The kid robber didn't like Peeps making jokes. I couldn't think of much else to say. Mrs. Dutton just had this angry look on her face. And Kate was too busy crying and sniffling to say anything.

Kate wasn't looking that good, either. Her makeup was running down her cheeks like black smudges. Her cheeks were pink, like she had a fever. And her forehead was wet with sweat. Right then, I doubted that any of us looked that good.

Then Al, the old robber came in. He was pushing the manager ahead of him.

"We gotta move," Al told the kid robber.

"You got the money?"

"In the briefcase. Maybe thirty, forty thousand."

"That's it?" asked the kid.

"What do you expect? You think this is a Brinks truck? It just a branch bank. They don't keep that much cash," Al said.

"So why did we even bother? That's nothing."

The two of them shot a look at each other. I wondered what kind of story the older guy had told the kid. I figured he talked him into this. But risking big prison time for half of thirty grand – that's just stupid. At some level, I think the kid knew it.

"Listen, we gotta move," said the old robber. "You see a car?"

"How am I supposed to see a car in here?" the young one snapped back.

"I'm just saying."

"And I'm just telling you. I ain't seen nothing."

The two robbers weren't getting along that well. They were having a fight like a married couple. It might have been funny – except it couldn't be. Two

guys with guns having a fight, and we were in the middle. A lousy place to be, I thought.

Then the phone rang.

This time, Al picked it up right away.

"Where's the freakin' car?" he barked into it.

I thought about the other end of the line. What if it was just some old lady calling to ask about her last deposit. What would she think?

But it was the cops. Once again, I could only hear one side of the phone call.

"You said half an hour. —— We did our side of the deal. You got the crying mom and we got nothing. So now what? —— No, I don't want to freakin' talk about this. I don't want no more deals. I want a car."

There was a long pause. I don't know what was coming from the other end.

Then Al started talking again.

"Doyle, I've heard all that before. I don't need it, man. I need a car, a clean car. Nobody following behind it. You deliver the car and then you get these nice people in here. Alive."

Again, silence.

"Excuses don't cut it, Doyle. I give you ten minutes, and then you get one more of these people. But he won't go walking out of here. He'll be falling out dead. You got that? A car in ten minutes, or you get your first dead hostage. That's the deal."

What a deal, I said to myself. Why didn't the cops just give them the car they wanted?

I looked at the clock on the wall. It was 3:30 p.m. On a school day, the little kids would be running out the doors. But this was Saturday. Peeps and me had been in the bank for not quite one hour, on the floor for half of that. The crying mom was out of here, picking up her kid from soccer practice. The rest of us were stuck. And one of us might soon be dead.

"Okay, you," the older robber said to Peeps. "Out by the door." He pointed his gun at my buddy, who already looked pretty scared.

"And then?" Peeps asked.

"You wait," Al told him. "Keep your eyes outside and don't try anything funny. If you make a move, remember I got a gun on you. And then we wait."

"For the car?" Peeps asked.

"Yeah, for the car."

Peeps went out to the glass front doors. Outside the bank, he must have seen police cars and yellow tape and all that. Inside, if he looked back, he'd see us on the floor of the office. And he could see the baseball bat.

Maybe Peeps was figuring the odds. What would happen if he ran for it? Probably get shot in the back. Or worse, the robbers would shoot Mrs. Dutton or Kate.

What would happen if he grabbed for the bat? It was out there, just by the office door. Peeps was pretty fast. If he had a chance, could he grab it and take down one of the robbers? And what would the other one do?

Chapter 6

Counting the Minutes

Ten minutes is a long time. Ten minutes is a long time anywhere. Even in school, waiting for the bell to ring, ten minutes can take forever.

When you're a hostage, ten minutes just crawls. Two guys with guns were ready to shoot. They were ready to shoot the bank manager, and maybe the rest of us. They'd try to shoot any cops that might try a rescue. They were crazy.

But Al had given the cops a deal, I told myself. All the cops had to do was get them a car. Then Al and the kid would let all of us go and they'd escape in the car. That's what half my mind said. It would be real simple, and I'd have a great story to tell at school.

But the other half of my mind saw a different ending. No car. A gunshot into Peeps' back. The cops shooting back. A bunch of us ending up dead. I didn't like the way that story played out.

We were all getting scared. I could see the bank manager, his leg twitching. Kate was crying again, but not making any noise. Mrs. Dutton had her head buried in her hands. Maybe she was praying.

There was no sound. Nothing from outside the bank. Nothing from inside. If clocks still ticked, we'd be listening to each tick. But modern clocks don't tick, they just go on and on.

And then there was a sound outside. A car pulled up in front of the bank, I was sure of it.

"The car is here," Peeps shouted from the other room.

"All right, get back in here," Al ordered.

The kid robber smiled. Al, the old robber, pulled out his cell phone.

Peeps came to the door. He looked kind of funny, and he was walking a bit stiffly.

"You," the kid robber shouted. "Whatcha doing?" He pointed his gun right at Peeps.

"Nothing," Peeps told him. He raised his hands in the air, as if that would do any good.

"So get in here," the kid told him.

But when Peeps started to walk, I could see the metal baseball bat sticking out of his pant leg. Peeps stopped and looked down. Then he froze, as if he was embarrassed. In a second, the bat was hitting the floor.

"Well look at this," Al said. "The guy is gonna take on both of us with a baseball bat."

The kid robber just laughed.

"Okay, Jose, kick it out. No time for baseball right now."

Peeps shook his leg and the bat fell to the floor. It made a hollow metal sound when it hit.

"Now walk over to the desk," the kid told Peeps. "Nice and slow. And then put your head down on the desk."

Peeps did what he was told. I could see my friend with his head on the desk. He was shaking from fear.

"Close your eyes," the kid ordered. "You don't want to see this coming."

Peeps did. His face was all tensed up, getting ready.

The rest of us were frozen, not sure what to do. This guy was going to kill my buddy, I was sure of it. But what could I do? If I tried to rush him he'd just shoot us both. It was hopeless.

The kid robber picked up the bat from the floor. He walked over to Peeps with a strange smile on his face. Then he lifted the bat.

The room was silent except for Peeps' breathing. His head was on the desk, the bat lifted over it. Time stopped.

With a grunt, the kid robber brought the bat down. I jumped and Kate looked away. But the bat didn't hit Peeps, it smashed into the manager's desk. A picture frame cracked into tiny bits of glass.

"Could have been your head," the kid robber said to Peeps. He looked around at all of us. It was as if he might raise the bat again and use it to hit any of us.

But he didn't have a chance. The desk phone rang. Al picked up.

"Yeah, I see it. —— Yeah, no problem. You can have some. —— No, you gotta be kidding. All of 'em? You think I'm freakin' crazy. —— You get some, we keep a couple until we're halfway to L.A. —— Nobody follows us, got it? No GPS tracking freakin' on the car. —— Good. We get away, and everybody stays alive. It's simple."

Al hung up the bank phone. Then he punched a

number on his cell phone. He must have been talking to the third guy in their gang.

"Okay, we're out of here in five minutes. . . . Yeah, we got the money. . . . Meet you like I said before. You know where."

Al punched the end button. Then he looked down at the four of us on the floor and Peeps by the desk.

"Okay, boys and girls, it's show time," he said. I think he was grinning, but it's hard to tell when a guy is wearing a stocking.

"So how does this work?" I asked. "You get in the car and we all wave goodbye, or what?'

Al shot me a look. "You know, kid, I don't like your mouth. I should shoot you some place where it hurts, just so you learn some freakin' respect.

"But I got a few other things to do first. So here's the deal. Everybody gets up and goes toward the front door. I'll be out by the counter with my gun on you. My buddy will be behind you. So don't try anything funny. That means you, wise guy." He pointed his gun at Peeps.

So we all got up. I had to help Kate, who was wobbly on her feet. Then we walked out to the main room of the bank and went toward the door. Outside the front door was a car – one of those basic cop cars with no markings.

"Okay, stop," the older robber ordered. It almost seemed like he'd done this before. "We're going out in two rows."

I felt like I was in gym class. Two rows or two lines? What did the guy want?

"Out in front, Mr. Manager. Then the old lady and the girl."

Mrs. Dutton and Kate got next to each other. They were both looking out at the street. There were cop cars out there, at least five of them. If they got that far, they were home free.

"Now, hero and baseball bat guy, you get behind them. Yeah, just like that."

So there we were: the manager at the door, the two girls behind him, Peeps and me behind them. And behind all of us were the robbers.

"Get your stocking on," Al said. He was giving orders to the young robber. "Bad enough these guys have seen your freakin' face. No sense showing the cops, too."

When the kid robber came back, he had the stocking over his head again.

"Okay, let's move," Al ordered. "Old guy, you go out first. Keep your hands up so the cops don't shoot you. Then the girls, but dead slow. Got me? No running."

"And what about us?" I asked.

"You two heroes are gonna be our freakin' protection," Al said. "You go out just in front of the kid and me. If the cops got a sharpshooter, he's gonna shoot you first. You get the idea?"

"Yeah, great," I said.

"You know how to drive a car, kid?" he asked me.

"Sure," I told him. That was kind of a lie, because I didn't have my license yet. I mean, I'm only fifteen. But I still knew how to drive. I'd been behind the wheel a couple of times with guys I know.

"Okay, so we get out there and you get behind the wheel. Smart mouth gets beside you. My buddy and I will get in the back and off we go."

"Off we go where?"

"Down the street. Then get on the highway."

Minor problem, I thought. I'd never driven on a highway. I'd only driven in a mall parking lot and on a couple of streets near my house. None of that was legal. And I didn't drive all that well, even then. But I figured it was the wrong time to mention it.

"Okay, everybody got the plan? If the cops don't go nuts, we'll all get out of here just fine."

I felt a gun barrel sticking in my back. I had a hunch that Peeps had another gun stuck into him.

"Okay, let's get some fresh air."

Chapter 7

Outside

When we first got outside, I could hardly see. The sun was so bright that I had to blink to get my eyes working. At last I saw the ring of cop cars. They had blocked all the streets except one. The getaway route.

If we got away at all.

The bank manager went first, hands up. Then Mrs. Dutton and Kate went out, hands up. I could see why the robbers sent them out first. They were a kind of human shield between us and the cops. There was no way the cops could risk shooting through them to get the bad guys.

Peeps and I were the next shield. Al was bigger than me, but he had ducked down so his head was at my level. Peeps and the young robber were the same size. The only way the cops could take a shot would be through me or through Peeps.

"Keep moving around the car," Al ordered.

The manager, Kate and Mrs. Dutton kept walking. Now Peeps and I were the only human shields, but the car was between us and the cops.

"Okay, hero, open the door and slide over behind the wheel," Al told me. "Mouthy guy gets in beside you."

I did what he said. The car had those old bench seats, so it was easy to slide over. I could hear Peeps get in after me. Then the two robbers got in behind us.

Outside, I could see Kate and Mrs. Dutton start to run toward the cops.

I held my breath. If the cops were going to start shooting, it would be now.

One second. Two seconds. No shots.

"Start the freakin' car," the old robber told me.

The keys were right there. With one shaking hand, I turned the keys and heard the starter grind. Nothing.

The young robber swore.

"If those cops . . ." Al began.

But I tried the key again. This time the engine

caught. I gave it a little gas, and got back a little roar. There wouldn't be much power in this thing, but it would go.

Outside, the police had put blankets around the bank manager, Kate and Mrs. Dutton. For them, the whole thing was over. For Peeps and me, it might just be beginning.

The car was an automatic. That was good, because I didn't know how to drive a stick shift. So I put the lever into D for drive, then began to go forward. That much was easy.

"Give it some juice," Al told me. He had ducked down to the floor, but his gun was still aimed at me. I had a hunch the kid in back had done the same. These guys were smart, I thought. No way the cops could get a clear shot at them.

I gave the car more gas and we pulled away from the bank. In front of me, I could see the one clear road. It would take us past the park where Peeps and I should have played baseball. It would take us by the school where we had learned to read. And then

it would take us onto the highway. That was the plan.

"Keep this thing moving," Al told me. "You don't stop for lights. You don't stop for nothing. Got it?"

"Yeah, I got it."

I wasn't driving very well. It kind of felt like a video game, maybe Crazy Taxi. The steering was kind of strange, and the brakes felt mushy. Still, I was doing okay. I'd slow down for lights, check for traffic, and then drive on through. It was kind of cool.

Finally, Al sat up. He must have figured the cops couldn't shoot him any more.

"Kid, you can't drive for. . . ."

"Thanks," I said.

It was white-knuckle driving. I was holding onto the steering wheel like my life depended on it. Good reason. My life did depend on it. I could feel the sweat pouring from my armpits. The sweat on my forehead was dripping down to my eyes and cheeks.

"Pretty hot in here," the kid robber said. "The freakin' cops left the heater on. Open your window up there."

That meant me. It also meant taking one hand off the steering wheel. I was sweating so much that the steering wheel was slippery in my grip.

"I can't," I told him. "I need two hands to steer this thing."

"You really know how to drive?"

"Yeah, kind of."

Peeps rolled down his window. That gave us a little air. The kid robber pulled off his stocking, and I thought old Al might do the same. I mean, a guy in a stocking in the middle of the summer kind of stands out. But no, he kept it on.

A cell phone rang. It didn't belong to the robber. It was in the glove box.

Nobody did a thing.

The cell phone kept ringing, stopped, then rang again.

This time, Al opened the glove box. He pulled out the phone, pressed a button, and listened.

Then he barked into the phone. "Yeah, Doyle. I figured it would be you. —— Nah, not interested in a deal. —— What's this? You wanna be my freakin' friend? —— Yeah, it's in the cop book on how to handle this. Keep the bad guys talking. Right? —— Yeah, but I don't want to talk."

Al rolled down his window. Then he threw the phone out onto the street. I couldn't see it smash, but I got the idea.

"Stupid freakin' cops," Al grumbled. "They always pretend to be on your side. Then you end up in court and forget the deals."

There wasn't much I could say on that. Peeps kept his mouth shut too.

"Okay, the highway's up ahead. You get on it and go south, then see how fast this thing will go."

"I thought you said I was a lousy driver," I told him.

My hands were gripping the wheel like crazy, and we were still on city streets.

"Yeah, I changed my mind," the robber said.

"I'm not so good on highways," I told him. Maybe I should have admitted the truth – I'd never driven on a highway. "We're not allowed. . . ."

"I'll tell you what you're allowed," the robber shot back.

"Hey, Rob, just don't kill us all," Peeps said in a low voice. "I'm too young to die."

"Yeah, me too," I said.

We'd made it to the on-ramp, then onto the highway. I put my foot to the floor and prayed.

Chapter 8

Run Like Crazy

"You trying to kill us, kid?" asked Al, the old guy.

"He really can't drive!" shouted the kid robber.

"It's the car," I told them. "The steering must be shot." That was a lie, of course. The steering wasn't great, but the problem was me. I was scared to death. The faster I went, the more scared I got. And then I started losing control.

"Slow it down and take the next exit," Al told me. "And don't roll us while you're at it."

I had actually thought about crashing the car. In the movies, the good guys always survive the crash and run away. The bad guys lose their guns and start dying.

But I figured that was just the movies.

I wondered if the cops were tracking us. It would be easy to do. Just plant a G P S someplace and send the info out. Then there was Boomerang! Put it in your car and it can show the cops where the car has gone. And then they can stop the car by remote control. Pretty cool stuff, but it wouldn't help us much. And it might make the two robbers angry. Who could tell what they'd do if they were angry.

I got us off the highway, alive. We were in some industrial park. There were factories and warehouses all around us

"Okay, so do what I tell you," Al said.

I almost said something back, but kept my mouth shut. Al had me making left and right turns like crazy. At one point, I thought we were going in circles. Then we got behind some factory called AB Farben, and he told me to stop.

"Gimme the keys," Al said. "My buddy is going to keep an eye on you two."

"Where are you going?" the kid robber asked.

"To get a new car," was the answer. "The cops will have a bug on this one, for sure."

He opened his door and went out, grabbing the briefcase.

It was hot. I rolled down the window.

"Hey, did I tell you to do that?" the kid robber asked.

"No, sorry. I'm kind of sweaty, that's all."

"Yeah, I can freakin' smell that." The kid robber began laughing again. He liked his own jokes.

"So what now?" Peeps asked.

"We get a new car," the kid replied. "Just like the boss said."

"And then you let us go," Peeps went on. It wasn't a question. More of a hope.

"Maybe," the kid said. "I don't know. I ain't done this kind of thing before."

"So Al tells you to jump, and you jump. Is that how it goes?" Peeps asked.

"Yeah, pretty much."

"So what do you get out of all this?" Peeps asked him. "Al's got the briefcase right now. He's got the money. You think he's coming back?"

"Shut up," the kid told him.

"Even if he does, you only get a third of the cash – or less. What's that come to, maybe five thousand bucks? This whole thing is a pretty big risk for that kind of money."

"I said shut up," the kid replied.

"I'm just saying, you could be up for robbery, assault and kidnapping. That's got to be twenty years' time, maybe thirty or forty."

"Only if I get caught," the kid robber said.

"Yeah, you won't ever get caught. You can trust Al to keep his mouth shut, right? And the third guy, the guy with the car. He won't talk, will he? These guys are your buddies. You can trust 'em." Peeps was really laying it on thick.

"Shut up."

"I'm just saying, you can cut your losses. You let us go, and we'll tell the cops that Al was behind the whole thing. He's got the money. And we'll say that you didn't want to take any hostages. We'll make it seem like you were a victim, just like us."

I wasn't sure if the kid robber was really listening.

"Listen, my name's Pedro and my buddy up there is Rob. What's your name, guy? Let's see if we can work something out."

"You don't need my freakin' name. Don't go trying anything."

Peeps didn't let up. "I just think a year in juvie beats twenty years in the pen. You haven't hurt anybody. Al did the real robbery. You were just in the wrong spot at the wrong time, that's all."

"You gonna be a freakin' lawyer?" the kid robber asked.

"Yeah, maybe," Peeps replied. "But Rob and I are both on your side. The guy behind all this is Al. He came up with the idea. He's the guy who hit the bank manager."

This was all true, of course. But was the kid getting it?

"You think he's looking out for you? You take the risk, but he gets most of the money. Maybe he gets all of the money. That's how it's going to play out, isn't it?"

I thought Peeps was doing a great job. He was doing what the cops always do in the movies – get onside with the kidnappers. Offer them a deal. Split up the partners. Offer them a better way out.

For a while, the kid robber was quiet. I thought he might be thinking about the whole thing. Maybe Peeps had worked a little magic. Maybe he'd let us go.

But no. That's not how it worked.

"You got a big mouth, Pedro. You want me to stick this gun into it?"

Peeps didn't get a chance to answer.

At that moment, an old Ford zoomed in front of us. The Ford backed up in a hurry. The driver's door flew open – and there was Al.

"Okay, everybody out," Al told us. He pulled his gun from his belt and aimed it at all of us. "Jamie, you watch these guys."

Ah, so the kid robber did have a name! Now we knew both of their names. I tucked it all away, just in case.

Peeps and I got out our side of the car. The kid robber, Jamie, got out his side. This was it, I said to myself. Surely they'd let us go. We'd been useful for a while, but now we were worth nothing. We weren't shields. We weren't anything. Just a couple of teenage kids who got in the way.

Then again, both Peeps and I had seen the kid's face. We knew both their names. We had seen everything they'd done. So maybe, just maybe . . . they'd kill us both.

I felt my knees go weak.

I looked around us, but there was nothing. The

walls of two warehouses, one on each side. A road that led to a blind turn. I hadn't seen a person or a car or a truck in fifteen minutes.

If Al shot us, we could bleed to death before anyone found us.

Or he could let us go. It could go either way.

"You, hero," he said, pointing his gun at me. "In the car. Back seat."

I did what he said, looking over at Peeps as I climbed into the car.

"You, big mouth," he said to Peeps. "You any good at running?"

"I . . . uh. . . ." I could see the fear in Peep's face.

"Just giving you a head start, big mouth," Al said. I thought he was smiling under the stocking. "You got five seconds before I put a bullet in a you."

Peeps was frozen. He got that deer-in-the-headlights look.

I tried to send a thought his way. Move!

"Four. . . ."

Peeps turned.

"Three. . . ."

And started running. Al pointed the gun at his back, taking aim.

"Two. . . ."

Peeps was zig-zagging. Al kept the gun on him.

"One. . . ."

Peeps was maybe thirty feet away. Not even the distance from home plate to first base.

"Bang!" Al shouted, and started to laugh.

Chapter 9

A Little Problem

"That was so freakin' funny," Al told Jamie. "I ain't seen a kid dance like that for years."

We were on the road again. Al was behind the wheel, his stocking pulled off. Now I could see his face – rough skin, small eyes, messed-up hair. He seemed to have a scar on one cheek, like he'd been cut with a knife.

"So you just let him go," Jamie replied.

"Yeah, but I scared the . . . out of him."

"What if he got the plate number?"

"He was too busy peeing his pants," Al replied. "By the time he gets to the cops, we'll be long gone."

"Like we planned."

"Yeah."

"Except," Jamie said, "we didn't get half a million bucks. We got maybe thirty thousand. How long are we gonna live on that?"

"Long enough," Al told him. "Now that you know how to do this, you'll see. It's easy. Lots of banks in this country."

We were back on the highway, heading into the desert. The sun was beating down, and it was hot. I could feel sweat dripping down my forehead and from my armpits.

I was in the back seat, trying to think. It was me up against two guys with guns. I had nothing – no baseball bat, no knife, no weapon. I didn't even have a cell phone. I could try to strangle one of them, but the other would shoot me. Or I could wait it out. These guys didn't want a murder charge. They'd might just let me go.

Or they might kill me. I knew too much. I'd seen too much.

That was the choice. Of course, they'd let Peeps go. They'd made him run like a fool, but they didn't kill him. They had no reason to kill me, either.

Unless something went wrong.

Something went wrong.

An hour later, we were driving down the highway. Now we were in the desert. The sun was blinding. The heat outside would make a snake curl up and die.

Al was driving pretty fast, way over the limit. I could see the speedometer from the back. We were going someplace, and we were going there in a hurry.

Then I heard a siren.

The cops, I thought. The cops are after us.

Both Al and Jamie started swearing. Jamie blamed Al. Al said it wasn't his fault. Both of them were wondering – had the cops traced us? Had my buddy Peeps given them the plate number? Were the cops bringing us down?

I looked back. It was only one cop car. Only one cop car with only one cop.

"It's nothing," Al said. He pulled the Ford off to the side of the road.

"It had better be nothing," Jamie replied. I heard him put the gun someplace up front.

Al turned around and looked at me.

"It's up to you, kid. You open your mouth and we have to shoot you . . . and shoot the freakin' cop. It kind

of raises the stakes for us, but you won't care about that. Because you'll be dead. You got the idea?"

"Yeah," I said. My voice was cracking a little. "So if I play along, you'll let me go."

"That's the deal, kid," Al told me. "It's pretty simple, ain't it?"

"Yeah, simple," I replied. My mouth felt dry.

The cop was sitting in his car behind us. I guess he was putting stuff into a computer. After a while, he got out of his car and walked toward us.

Al put down the window. The hot desert air began pouring into the car.

"Yes, sir," Al said, as polite as could be. "What could I do for you?"

"Let me see your license and registration," the cop said. He was a young guy, maybe twenty-five or thirty.

Al handed over his driver's license. Jamie got the registration from the glove box. They handed them to the cop. The cop took both pieces back to his car, and then we waited.

"He's gonna see your record," Jamie said.

"Shut up and keep smiling," Al replied. "Those cop cars have a camera on us. Don't you ever watch TV?"

"Yeah, I watch a lot of freakin' TV. The problem is you, Al. He's gonna see that you spent some time."

"So?" Al replied. "The car's clean and I'm clean. I paid for what I did. Not like you, with all your time in juvie."

"Yeah, yeah."

The cop came back. He leaned down at the window. I think he was checking Al's breath to see if he'd been drinking.

"You know you were over the limit," the cop said.

"The ticket would cost you about $180."

"I'm sorry officer," Al told the cop. "But my buddy here," he pointed at Jamie, "he's got some stomach trouble. I got to get him to a bathroom, if you know what I mean."

"Is that right?" he asked Jamie.

"Yes, sir," Jamie told him. He was thinking fast. "I think it was something I ate."

"That can happen," the cop said. "There's a gas station up ahead, maybe twenty minutes."

"Thank you," Jamie said. "I really need it."

"And what about you back there?" the cop asked. He was looking back at me.

So it was my choice. I could have said something. I could have whispered "help me" or "get out your gun and arrest these guys." But I didn't. I just looked at him and tried to find a voice.

"I'm feeling okay," I lied.

"You don't look so good," the cop told me.

"Yeah, well, I get a little car sick sometimes," I said. That much was true.

So the cop turned back to Al.

"See the speed limit sign up there?" the cop said. "That's for everybody. Even guys with bad stomachs.

You stay under that and I'll let you go this time. But if I see you speeding again, I'm not just writing a ticket, I'm running you in. You understand that?"

"Yes, sir," Al said. "Thank you."

"Thanks a lot officer," Jamie added. He was smiling for once. I noticed he had bad teeth.

I said nothing. I didn't know if I'd been smart or stupid. I didn't know if I'd saved the life of a young cop – and maybe my life – or blown my last chance to get free. But I felt lousy. And I felt stupid.

Al rolled up the window. Jamie reached somewhere and got his gun.

"You did good, kid," Al told me.

That gave me an idea. "Yeah, but I've got a little problem," I told him. "How about we make a stop at that gas station?"

Chapter 10

Last Chance

Okay, I'd done my bit. I'd said nothing to the cop. I hadn't blown the whistle. I hadn't cried for help. Now it was Al and Jamie's turn.

Or maybe it was my turn. Maybe I could get a message to somebody while we stopped at the gas station. Maybe I could get them to send help. Not one cop, but a dozen cops. If I could find a piece of paper, maybe, and a pencil.

I started looking around the back seat. Nothing.

Meanwhile, the guys in front were talking.

"I say we stop," Jamie said. "I could use a bathroom break, and maybe some food."

"And give the kid a chance to run?" Al asked.

"He won't run," Jamie told him. "Rob's on our side. He showed you back there with the cop."

"Rob is it?" Al snapped back at his partner. "How come you know the kid's name? Are you guys best buddies all of a sudden? What's going on here?"

"I'm just saying . . ."

"And I'm just telling you. I run this thing, not you," Al told him. "I got the experience. This kid, this kid's got nothing more to give us."

"So what's that mean?" Jamie asked.

"It means, we should get rid of him. Ditch him."

"Where?"

"Not at a freakin' gas station. The kid knows too much. He's gonna be a problem."

"So where?"

"Some place like right over there."

I could feel Al putting on the brakes. He made a turn off the highway onto some smaller road. I could hear the gravel under the tires. A few minutes later, Al brought the car to a stop.

"Okay, hero. Out you go."

I looked outside the car window. There was nothing – just desert. I mean, there was sand and some cactus plants, but that was it. Desert.

"Come on," I said. "We had a deal." I was scared like anything. Part of me wanted to cry.

Al laughed. Then he opened his door and got out of the car. A second later, he pulled open my door. The desert heat came rushing in. It felt like a million degrees.

"Al, I don't know about this," Jamie said.

Al ignored him.

"Out," he told me. "Or I'll drag you out."

I got out of the car. Jamie got out of his side. Now all three of us were out under the desert sun. It was maybe five o'clock. The sun would be beating down for another three hours. I could be fried by then. I could have gone crazy from the sun by then. I could be dead by then.

"You can't do this," I said. "There's no shade. There's nothing. I could be dead before the sun sets."

"Hey, come on," Al told me. "I thought you were the hero type. It's a little hot, maybe. A little dry. But you'll make it. Somebody will find you tomorrow."

"Somebody will find my body," I said to him.

Then I got smart. There was no sense begging Al for anything. He didn't care about me . . . or much of anything. But Jamie was my age. Jamie might really care about what would happen next. Jamie was my only chance.

"Jamie, if I die out here, you're going up for murder. Think about that." Get onside with them, that's the advice. Don't be a victim, be a real person.

"He's got a point, Al," Jamie said.

"Shut up, kid," Al barked. I don't know if he was talking to Jamie or to me. It didn't matter. I had to keep talking or I'd end up dead.

"Jamie," I told him, "it doesn't matter if Al shoots me or if I die from thirst, it's still murder. And you're in on it. Rob a bank, and maybe the cops won't care. But you kill me out here, the cops will hunt you down. Then it's murder one, Jamie."

I didn't really know much about murder charges. I guess there are different kinds. Murder one sounded good, like something from a movie.

"Al, I didn't sign up to kill anybody," Jamie said.

"We're not killing anybody. We're just leaving him out here," Al replied.

"With no water and no shade. It's a freakin' desert, Al, in case you weren't paying attention."

"I know what a freakin' desert is, kid."

"Yeah, and what if he dies?" Jamie asked.

Al didn't say anything. The question kind of hung up there, in the air.

"I don't want to go down for murder, Al," Jamie told him. "I didn't sign up for that. I didn't sign up for any of this kidnapping stuff."

Then it was quiet. Al and Jamie were staring at each other. Then Al lifted his gun and aimed it at Jamie.

"Toss down your gun, kid."

Jamie looked stunned. This was his buddy. This was the guy who talked him into robbing a bank. And now Al's gun was aimed at his head.

"Just toss it on the ground," Al said. His voice was gentler this time.

Jamie threw out his gun. It landed on the sand without a sound.

"You, hero," he said, talking to me. He seemed to have the gun on both of us. "You kneel down right here."

"Kneel down?" I asked.

"Yeah, like you're praying. You know? Like you were in a freakin' church. You kneel down and look at the cactus over there."

"Al, what are you doing?" Jamie asked.

"I'm doing what we gotta do," Al snapped back.

"You keep your stupid mouth out of this." He stopped. It was quiet.

By then, I was kneeling on the ground. I was ready for the bullet – at least, I think I was. I figured it would be one bullet in my brain. At least I'd die quick. If I was going to die, I wanted it quick.

"Hero," Al said, "what am I going to do with you?" I think he was asking himself more than me. "A bullet in your head gets rid of the big witness. But then I'm up for murder. Maybe Jamie too." It was like he was talking through the whole thing. "But if I leave you here, maybe you die anyway. Wouldn't you rather go quick than slow?"

I didn't answer. I was kneeling on the sand, my eyes looking at nothing. I wished I knew how to pray. It would have been a good time to pray.

I heard a click from behind me. Al took the safety off his gun.

And then, something happened. I couldn't see it. All I could do was hear it.

There was a scuffing sound, feet moving. Then something hit the sand. Then there was a pause, maybe a second. And then there was a gunshot.

I froze.

Was I hit? Did a bullet come into me? Was I going to die like this? Was I going to bleed to death in the desert?

No. None of that. I heard swearing from behind me. It was Al, swearing a blue streak.

"Why'd you freakin' do that, you. . . . Why'd you shoot me, you freakin' . . . ?"

I turned around. Somehow Jamie had his gun back. Somehow he'd shot Al right in the hand – right in the hand that held the gun.

"'Cuz I don't want to go down for murder, Al. I didn't sign up for that."

Chapter 11

In the End

Nobody got hurt much when it was all over. The bank manager needed some dental work. Al, the old robber, needed a little work on his hand. But Jamie was a good shot. The bullet hit the gun first, then bounced into Al's hand. The damage wasn't that bad. Al might have trouble making a fist ever again, but that's not a bad thing.

But a lot of things changed that day at the bank. For one thing, Peeps and I became kind of heroes. The newspaper stories made us seem cool and brave. They said we saved the lives of Mrs. Dutton and Kate. The newspapers said I had talked the "hostage takers" out of further shootings. They said we kept our nerve all the way through. They said we deserved some kind of medal. In fact, the mayor called my mom and said we might really get a medal.

Pretty cool, eh? Except it wasn't quite like that. We weren't quite the cool and heroic guys that the papers said. Now you know what happened, you can judge for yourself.

When the court case came up, Peeps and I were on Jamie's side. He'd gone along for a bank robbery, but none of the rest was supposed to happen. He was as scared as we were – scared of Al, scared of the cops, scared of everything. He was just looking for a little quick cash, not a life of crime.

And that's what we told the judge. Jamie didn't hurt anybody. Jamie didn't plan the hostage taking. Al was the boss; Jamie was on our side all along. (Okay, maybe not all along, but that was our story.) And at the end, Jamie saved my life. Al was going to kill me, and Jamie shot the gun right out of his hand.

It made a great story. We even made the national news. I had TV crews trying to talk to me. But Peeps got smart. He said they had to pay for an interview. Most of the TV guys backed off, but one station came up with cash. A lot of cash.

So now my bank account has $5481 and some interest. I'm pretty close to that car I had in the back of my mind. Except I've got a new idea about school – like actually working at it. Maybe there's a good job out there for me. Maybe if I go back to school and actually study, I could learn something. Maybe.

Peeps, of course, can always play baseball. But now he's thinking about college and law school. Ever since Jamie told him he should be a lawyer, he's got this idea in his head. So maybe it'll work out like that. I can see Peeps as a lawyer, or a baseball player, or both. You never know.

The old robber, Al, was a three-time loser. I don't think he'll ever get out of jail this time. Maybe that's fair. At least nobody has to worry about him for a while.

And Jamie got probation. I could hardly believe it. I figured – given all the charges – he'd get some juvie time. But no. I guess his rescue of me really impressed the judge. (It sure impressed me.) So Jamie is back in high school, trying to graduate.

Just like me, I guess.

Except that I'm famous – kind of. Lots of people in town nod their heads at me. Mrs. Dutton treats me like I'm a long lost son. The bank manager wants to give me a credit card. And Kate. . . .

I wish I could say that Kate was so impressed that she fell in love with me. I wish I could say that Kate – despite being five years older and fifty times better looking – fell for this pimply high school kid. But that would be a lie.

Kate quit the bank and married her boyfriend.

Bummer.

But I'm taking driving lessons now. Lots of girls like me. And the future looks pretty good. Any kind of future looks good after you've been kneeling in the desert waiting for a bullet.

Quake

by ALEX KROPP

When the first earthquake hits, Cyrus is still at home. He leads his sister to safety, then heads to the local hospital to help other victims. That's when the aftershock hits – the second quake that buries him alive.

Lost

by SHARON JENNINGS

Rafe Reynolds thought it would be easy to lead a group of kids into wilderness camping. But soon he's lost in the woods with one of the campers. Together they have to deal with everything from bears and broken bones to anger and fist fights. It all threatens their survival.

Overboard

by E.L. THOMAS

An accident at sea leaves Tanner in a lifeboat with his kid sister and a guy he really despises. The survival of the group depends on their working together. But as the hot sun beats down and the water runs out, their chances don't look good.

Wave

by D.M. OUELLET

Luke and Mai could see the tsunami coming at them, but that didn't give them enough time to get away. When the wave hit, they fought to breathe and fought to reach dry land. And that was only the beginning of the disaster.

Frozen

by LORI JAMISON

Frank and Ray are stranded in the Arctic. Their snowmobile is broken and no one knows where they are. An Arctic storm is coming that can freeze them to death in minutes. The question is simple: how can they survive?

Alex Kropp is the author of *Hacker* (HIP Sr. series), *Turf War* (HIP Edge series) and *Quake* (HIP Xtreme). He has done editorial work for a number of publishers and now works in product development for Research In Motion.

For more information on HIP novels:

High Interest Publishing
www.hip-books.com